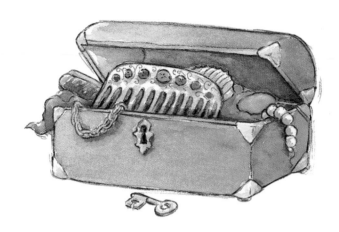

This book belongs to:

Leeann Kathryn Freund

Love Mommy !

A Treasury for

Six

Year Olds

A Treasury for

Six
Year Olds

A Collection of Stories,
Fairy Tales, and Nursery Rhymes

p

Illustrated by Rory Tyger (Advocate)

Designed by Peter Lawson
Series design by Zoom Design

Language consultant: Betty Root

This is a Parragon Publishing book
This edition published in 2003

Parragon Publishing
Queen Street House
4 Queen Street
Bath BA1 1HE, UK

ISBN 0-75258-712-9
Printed in China

◆ Contents ◆

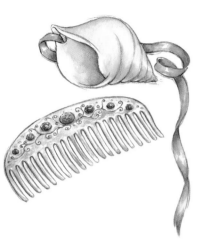

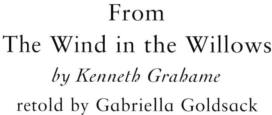
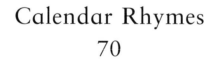

11

The Comb and the Trumpet Shell

Every summer, Lucie and her family went to stay in a cottage by the ocean. Lucie loved the seashore. Each day when the tide went out, she hunted for treasures in the sand.

One day Lucie found a pearly white shell with pink and silver speckles.

One day she found a smooth egg-shaped stone that was the color of sunset.

One day she found an old coin with a king's head on it.

Lucie took all her treasures back to the cottage and put them in a shoebox that she

12

kept under her bed.

Most afternoons, Lucie's mom and dad and her brother Joe went swimming in the ocean. Lucie went with them, but she would only get her feet wet.

"It's too cold today," she would say. Or, "Maybe tomorrow. Today I'll just watch you."

It wasn't that she couldn't swim. Lucie loved to swim in the pool at school. But the ocean was deep and dark and busy, and full of scary secrets.

One morning, as Lucie walked by the shore, she saw something sparkling in the sand. She crouched down to see what it was.

It was a comb! A shiny silver comb, with sparkling green and purple jewels set along the top. Lucie turned it over and over in her hand, wondering how

anything could be so beautiful. Then she ran home to put it in her treasure box.

The next morning, when Lucie was out treasure hunting, she heard a strange noise. As she listened carefully, she realized it was the sound of someone crying.

Lucie looked around, and saw a little girl bobbing

gently in the water. Her long golden hair drifted out behind her, gleaming in the sunlight. The girl was sobbing as if her heart was broken in pieces.

"Hello," called Lucie softly. "My name's Lucie. What's the matter?"

"My name's Meriel," said the little girl, "and I've lost my comb. It used to belong to my grandmother, and it's very, very precious. I thought I dropped it near

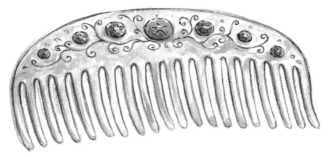

here yesterday, but now I can't find it anywhere!"

Lucie's face felt red and hot, and her tummy turned to jelly. "Is your comb silver, with green and purple jewels along the top?" she asked.

"Yes!" said Meriel. "Yes, it is! Have you seen it?"

"Yes," said Lucie very quietly. She felt tears stinging her eyes. "I found it. If you come back to my cottage, I'll give it to you."

"I can't come with you," said Meriel.

"Why not?" asked Lucie.

"Look," said Meriel. And out of the water flashed a splendid, gleaming, silvery-greeny-purply-pink tail.

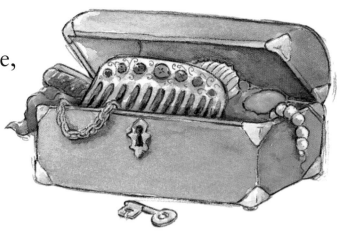

"Ohhhh!" whispered Lucie, her eyes wide with wonder. Then she turned and rushed back to the cottage. Five minutes later she was back, holding her treasure box.

"Here," she said to Meriel, holding out the comb. "It's the best treasure I ever found, but I'm glad you'll have it back now."

"Thank you!" said Meriel. "Thank you so much!" As she slid the comb into her golden hair, she looked up at Lucie.

"I can't come to your home, but would you like to see mine?" she asked.

Lucie looked at the deep, dark ocean. Then she looked at Meriel.

"I don't think so," she said,

shaking her head. "But thank you anyway."

"Please?" said Meriel, holding out her hand. "It's so beautiful, and I'll look after you, I promise! Please come with me, just for a little while."

Lucie put one toe in the water. Then her whole foot. Gently, Meriel took her hand and guided her down, down, down below the surface.

What a sight met Lucie's eyes! It wasn't dark at all! The water was filled with shimmering lights and sparkling colors. Gold and silver starfish twinkled on the ocean floor, and seahorses pranced around her. Clam shells and oyster shells glistened pink and white.

Sleek little rainbow-colored fish darted here and there, and crabs and lobsters clicked "hello" with their claws.

"All these are my friends," said Meriel. "Now they're your friends, too."

Lucie and Meriel swam through cascades of lacy seaweed until they came to a coral cave.

"This is where I live," said Meriel. "Wait here. I want to get something for you."

She glided into the cave and came out with a little shell shaped like a trumpet. It shone softly, and had a tiny hole at the top. Meriel strung it on a ribbon of seaweed and tied it around Lucie's neck.

"It's a gift from me—and the ocean," she said. "Now the ocean will always be a part of you, and you will be a part of it. Just like me."

"Thank you," whispered Lucie.

Meriel took Lucie's hand, and they swam back to the surface together. When they reached the place where they had met, Meriel said, "I have to say goodbye now, but I will always remember you. Thank you for finding my comb and keeping it in a safe place."

"And thank you for my trumpet shell," said Lucie. "I will wear it always, to remind me of you."

That afternoon, when Mom and Dad and Joe went swimming, Lucie went with them. Her trumpet shell sparkled, and she laughed as she skimmed through the tumbling waves.

And when she looked out toward the horizon, Lucie was sure she caught a glimpse of golden hair flashing in the sunlight.

The Pied Piper of Hamelin

Hamelin was a lovely little town, full of narrow, cobbled streets and wood-framed houses. The people who lived there had a very good life. However, they weren't at all happy. They weren't happy because their town was overrun with rats.

Thousands and thousands of rats swarmed the streets and ran through the houses. They raided pantries, ransacked trash, ate through doorways and walls, frightened children—and even attacked the town's cats. They were everywhere—even in beds and bathtubs! Something had to be done.

After the townspeople had tried everything, from poisons and potions to rat traps and rat cats, they began to despair. One afternoon, they gathered together and marched to the mayor's house.

"Enough is enough," cried the crowd. "The rats are eating our food and making our children sick. The rats must go, or we will make sure that you do."

"Good people," smiled the mayor. "I will not rest until our town is rid of this deadly plague of rats. This very afternoon I will send out a proclamation offering 100 gold coins to anyone who can rid this town of rats. It will be a small price for us to pay."

And so the mayor issued his proclamation. In the following days, all kinds of people arrived in Hamelin to try their hand at getting rid of the rats. There were magicians and merchants, soldiers and scientists. But one after another, each one gave up and returned home.

21

Then, just as the mayor was about to give up hope, a stranger knocked on the door of the town hall. A very odd-looking fellow, wearing a colorful patched cloak and a pointed hat, stood in front of the mayor. In his hand, the stranger carried a long musical pipe.

"What is your business?" asked the mayor, frowning at the man and his pipe. "This isn't a good time. The town is much too busy with rats to be bothered with music."

"Aha! Well, I'm your man," laughed the stranger. "I can get rid of all your rats before nightfall."

The mayor secretly thought that the stranger looked a bit peculiar, but out loud he said, "You certainly look like the man for the job.

As soon as the rats are gone I will hand over 100 gold coins. By the way, what is your name?"

"I am the Pied Piper," said the stranger. Then he was gone.

The Pied Piper walked to the main street. He put his pipe to his lips and began to play a haunting melody. Before he had played more than a handful of notes, there was a rumbling sound, and a huge swarm of rats appeared. Rat after rat streamed after the mysterious piper as he walked through the narrow streets, playing his magical tune.

The rats poured out of houses, holes, gutters, barns, ditches, and workshops. They followed the stranger on and on, until he came to a fast-running stream. Then, as the piper stood at the water's

edge, all the rats plunged into the water and drowned.

The people of Hamelin were overjoyed. Church bells rang out all over the town, and the townspeople quickly arranged a street party to celebrate.

As the whole town danced around in celebration, the Pied Piper appeared before the mayor.

"What now?" said the mayor, frowning at the odd-looking fellow.

"My 100 gold coins, if you please?" said the Pied Piper, holding out his hand.

But the mayor just laughed. "You want 100 gold coins for tricking a few silly rats with a pipe. Anyone could do that. Besides, the rats have drowned. There's no way you can bring them back. I tell you what, I'll give you 50 gold coins. Isn't that generous?"

"Yes, yes," shouted the townspeople, who seemed to have quickly forgotten the misery that the rats had brought. "Fifty gold coins is more than he deserves. Why, he's little more than a beggar!"

"I have kept my side of the bargain," said the Pied Piper. "Now I want payment in full. If you won't hand it over, I will be forced to play a tune that this whole town will live to regret."

"Keep this up and you won't get a penny," cried the mayor. And the townspeople all quickly agreed that the stranger should get nothing at all.

Without saying another word, the Pied Piper walked to the outskirts of town, where he put his pipe to his lips and began to play his haunting melody. The adults stood spellbound as the town's children stopped what they were doing and skipped after the piper. Laughing, the boys and girls scrambled down steps and up hills, just as the rats had.

The mayor and the townspeople looked on helplessly as the Pied Piper headed for the stream where the rats had drowned. They let out a sigh of relief when he used the bridge to cross to the other side, then headed uphill toward a large mountain. All this time the children were following him.

"There's no way they can get over that mountain," said the mayor. "He'll have to bring them back."

However, the mayor was wrong. When the Pied Piper got to the mountain, he played a few special notes and an opening appeared in the hillside. The Piper slipped through, and the children followed him. Then the opening closed, and the only thing that could be

heard was a distant sobbing. It was a small boy, crying because he was too slow and had been left behind.

Later, the small boy told the townspeople how the Pied Piper had promised to take the children to a wonderful kingdom of laughter and games, where they could all live happily forever. The mayor and his people didn't know whether to believe the story, but they never saw the children again.

From that day on, the sound of children's laughter was never heard in the sad streets of Hamelin again. How the people wished that they had kept their promise to the Piper.

In the Dark, Dark Wood

In the dark, dark wood,

there was a dark, dark house,

And in that dark, dark house,

there was a dark, dark room,

And in that dark, dark room,

there was a dark, dark closet,

And in that dark, dark closet,

there was a dark, dark shelf,

And on that dark, dark shelf,

there was a dark, dark box,

And in that dark,

dark box, there was a

GHOST!

Three Little Ghosties

Three little ghosties,
Sitting on posties,
Eating buttered toasties,
Greasing their fisties,
Up to their wristies,
Oh, what beasties,
To make such feasties!

The Dragon and the Unicorn

High up in the misty mountains lived the last dragon on Earth. Once upon a time, he had had many friends and relatives. But over the years they had all vanished. Now he was all alone.

Dragon was tired of being lonely, so he decided it was time to fly down the mountainside and look for some company. He spread his mighty wings, and flew through the clouds and mists, down . . .

down . . .

and down . . .

until he came to a deep, green forest.

30

Dragon folded his wings and went exploring. All was still among the tall, leafy trees until Dragon heard a rustling nearby. Suddenly, among the shadows, he spied something shimmering silvery white. A moment later, a gentle-looking creature with a long horn on its head came toward him.

"Hello," said Dragon. "Who are you?"

"I'm a unicorn," said the creature. "And you must be a dragon. Long ago, my grandfather told me stories about dragons."

Dragon looked sad. "All the other dragons are gone now. I'm the only one left," he said.

"I'm the last of my kind, too," said Unicorn. "Grandfather told me that people stopped believing in creatures like us. And when they stopped believing, they

stopped seeing us, even when we were right there in front of their eyes. When people stop seeing us, we vanish."

"If that's really what happened," said Dragon, "then it won't be long before you and I vanish, too!"

"Yes," said Unicorn, "unless . . ."

". . . unless we find someone who believes in us, and can see us," said Dragon.

"What are we waiting for?" asked Unicorn. "We'd better start looking!"

So, together, the two new friends traveled out of the forest and down a long, twisting road. After a long time, they came to a busy, crowded town. There were people everywhere, but no one paid any attention to Dragon or Unicorn. Even when they bumped into the creatures, the people just muttered and kept walking.

"I don't think they can see us," said Dragon.

"No," agreed Unicorn. "But we have to keep looking."

A little way outside the town, they saw a castle with tall towers and a huge wooden door. At the top of the towers brightly colored flags and banners fluttered in the breeze.

"I remember Grandfather telling me about princesses who lived in castles," said Unicorn excitedly. "They used to come to the forest to look for unicorns."

"Yes!" said Dragon. "I remember hearing about princesses too, and dragons who kept them locked up in towers. Then brave knights would come and fight the dragons. Oh, they sounded like such exciting times!"

"There must be someone inside the castle who believes in us," said Unicorn. "Let's go inside."

Inside the castle's great hall, they saw more flags and banners. To their delight, one of the flags was decorated with pictures of them!

"This is definitely the right place!" said Dragon.

They came to the banqueting hall. There, around a long table, men and women sat eating and drinking

and laughing. Among them sat a young and beautiful girl. When she laughed it sounded like a crystal stream skipping over stones.

"I'm sure she's a princess," whispered Unicorn. "I'll just go over so that she can see me."

But even when Unicorn stood right beside her, the beautiful young woman didn't see him. She just kept laughing and talking to the young man beside her. Unicorn nuzzled her shoulder, and the young woman turned around, but all she said was, "Oh, how

strange. I thought someone tapped me on the shoulder!" She never saw Unicorn at all.

Dragon, meanwhile, wasn't having any better luck at the other side of the table. He was dancing around beside a tall, handsome man who looked as if he might be a brave knight—but the man didn't notice him at all. In desperation, Dragon sent a blast of his fiery breath over the table.

"It's suddenly very warm, isn't it?" said the man, loosening his collar.

"Yes, you're right," said the woman sitting next to him. "I'll get someone to damp down the fire." And she called to a servant standing near the door. No one saw Dragon at all.

Unicorn came trotting over to him. "It's no use," he said sadly. "They can't see us, because they just don't believe that we're here." With their hearts heavy and sad, the two friends left the castle.

"I imagine that we'll vanish soon," said Unicorn, "just the way all our friends and relatives have."

35

"Yes," sighed Dragon. "At least we have each other for company until then." Slowly the two set off back toward the dark forest.

Suddenly, outside a small house just down the road from the castle, Dragon and Unicorn heard voices. They stopped to listen.

"Help! Help, Sir Knight!" someone was shouting. "Save me and this gentle unicorn!"

"Fear not, fair damsel!" another voice replied. "I will slay the fierce dragon!"

Dragon and Unicorn looked at one another, hardly daring to believe their ears. Slowly and quietly, they followed the voices to a yard behind the small house. There they saw a girl and a boy, playing with a toy horse and a wooden sword and shield. Holding their breath, Dragon and Unicorn took a few steps closer.

"William, look!" gasped the girl. "A real unicorn!"

"And Sarah, there's a real dragon, too!" cried William excitedly. "I've always wanted to see one, and now my wish has come true!"

Leaving their toys, the children ran up to the pair.

"You're real! You're real!" they shouted gleefully. "Will you stay and play with us? Will you stay with us always?"

Dragon and Unicorn felt their hearts swell with joy. At last they had found two people who believed in them. As Unicorn galloped across the garden with Sarah on his back, and Dragon playfully reared up so William could attack him, they both knew that this was where they belonged. As long as the children were here, they would be here too.

The Selfish Giant

There was once a beautiful garden that belonged to a giant. The giant had traveled far away many years earlier, but nature had cared for his garden. It was carpeted with soft green grass and decorated with lovely flowers. Peach trees stood over it. In the spring they burst into delicate blossom, in autumn they bore golden fruit. Birds sat in the trees and sang sweetly all day long.

TRESPASSERS WILL BE YELLED AT!

Every day, after school, children would play in the giant's garden. They sat in the trees and danced through the grass. The giant's garden was such a happy place. Then, one winter's day, the giant returned from his travels. "What are you doing in my garden?" he growled at the children, and away they ran.

"What nerve!" grumbled the giant. "Imagine coming into my garden without being invited. From now on it will just be me playing in here." Then he built a high wall around the garden and put up a sign saying, "TRESPASSERS WILL BE YELLED AT!"

The children had nowhere to play, but the giant didn't care. What a selfish giant!

Then spring arrived. All over the country, the trees blossomed, the flowers bloomed, and the birds sang. But in the giant's garden, it was still winter. No birds had visited since the children had been driven away, and now the trees refused to blossom. Even the flowers couldn't be bothered to wake up from their winter's sleep.

Snow and Frost were delighted. "We can live here all year round," they said. Snow covered the grass with her thick white blanket. Frost painted the trees silver. Then they invited their friends North Wind and Hail to stay.

North Wind raced around the garden and thrashed at the giant's house. He knocked bricks from the chimney and swept shingles off the roof.

Hail thudded down on the giant's house all day long, every day. How the miserable giant wished they would all go away.

Spring never arrived in the giant's garden that year, and neither did summer or fall. They all thought the giant was too selfish.

Then, one morning, the giant was wrapped up in bed when he heard some beautiful music. It took him a while to figure out that it was bird song. It had been so long since he had heard any. Before long, Hail stopped and the North Wind died down. Then a delicious, flowery smell wafted through a crack in the window.

"Hooray!" cried the selfish giant. "I think that perhaps spring has arrived at last." He peeked out of the window to see.

In the garden, a wonderful sight met his eyes. The children had climbed through a hole in the wall and were sitting in the branches of the trees. The trees were so pleased to see their old friends that they had burst into blossom. The birds were singing with joy, and the flowers had popped up their heads to see what all the fuss was about. The garden was beautiful once more.

There was just one corner where winter remained. Beneath a tree stood a small boy. He was crying because he was not tall enough to reach the tree's branches. Frost and Snow still covered the tree, while the North Wind and Hail raged above it.

As the giant watched the weeping boy, his heart began to thaw.

"I've been so selfish," he thought. "Now I know why spring would not come to my garden. I will go out and help that poor boy."

So the giant rushed out into the garden to help. When the children saw him, they were scared and ran away. Winter returned to the garden at once. Only the small boy, who was too busy crying to notice the giant, remained.

The giant crept over to the boy and gently lifted him up into the tree. Snow, Frost, Hail, and North Wind disappeared in a flash. The tree burst into blossom, and birds flew over and began to sing.

The boy was so grateful that he leaned down and kissed the giant. The giant's heart melted.

When they saw that the giant was no longer grumpy, the other children quickly returned to the garden, and with them came spring.

The giant was delighted. He took out a huge ax and, with a few hefty blows, knocked down the wall around the garden.

"This garden is yours now," he told the children. "Play here whenever you wish. I now see that being selfish only leads to unhappiness."

When the villagers passed by on their way home from work, they were surprised to see the children playing in the most beautiful garden they had ever seen. They were even more surprised to see the giant playing with them. Everyone was delighted that the selfish giant had given up his wicked ways.

A Drink for
Draggle Dragon

On a hot, hot day, the only thing a grown-up dragon wants to do is to crawl into her cool, dark cave and have a long snoooooooozzze. Lovely!

But little dragons are just like you and me. They don't want to sleep on a beautiful afternoon. They want to whizzzzzz around the mountain paths, and zoooooom over the rocks and sliiiiiide down the slopes.

One day, after whizzing and zooming and sliding under the sizzling hot sun, Draggle Dragon flopped down on the mountainside. What he needed more than anything else was a long, cool drink.

Down in the valley, sparkling in the sunshine, was a deep mountain lake. Under the surface, the water was dark and cold. A drink of it would be delicious.

Draggle sighed. He remembered what his mother had told him, over and over again.

"Never," she always said, looking serious and stern, "drink anything but juniper juice. And drink it through a straw. That is the only safe drink for dragons."

It was a long way back to the cave and the juniper juice.

Draggle crept down a winding path, closer and closer to the cold, blue water. As he watched, some little birds skimmed over the water's surface, dipping

their beaks to take a drink. Surely, if little birds could drink the water, it would be safe for a dragon!

Draggle went right up to the edge of the lake. He dipped one toe in the water. Ooooh! It was lovely! And nothing bad happened to his toe at all.

"Excuse me!" said a polite little voice. And a small deer trotted around the side of Draggle and began to drink from the lake.

Tiny birds could drink the water. Delicate deer could drink the water. Draggle made up his mind. He couldn't think of a single reason why he shouldn't drink it, too.

The naughty little dragon cupped his paws and scooped some water toward his mouth. Most of it dripped out between his claws, but a few precious, sparkling drops went in. It was sooooo good.

Nothing horrible happened. But it would take ages to drink a lot this way. Draggle decided to risk it. He leaned forward and dipped his face in the lake. And as the clear, cold water rushed into his mouth, something horrible did happen.

Pffffft!

Draggle's flames went out! All dragons breathe fire. They are so used to it that they don't even think about it. But they are careful when they walk through the forest, and dragons don't have curtains in their caves!

Pffffft!

Draggle breathed hard. He thought his flames might come back. But they didn't. He tried coughing and sneezing and shaking his head. It didn't work.

As he ran home, he began to panic. What would his mother say?

She said a lot. Some of the politer words she used were "Dunklebrain," "Google," and "Durkdragon."

Draggle waited until she paused. "Is there anything we can do?" he asked in a tiny voice.

Draggle's mother sighed. "It's dangerous. It's unpleasant. And it serves you right," she said. "We have to go to the volcano."

The journey to the volcano was long and tiring. And a journey always feels longer when your mother is muttering about you the whole way. But there are worse things than muttering. A roaring mountain spitting out stones and red-hot fire is worse, for starters.

Draggle was very frightened of the volcano.

"Stop whimpering, Draggle," said his mother. "This is what we must do. We fly over the top—quickly, of course—and, as we pass over the big hole in the middle, you must take a big breath in. That will light up your flames again."

Draggle had never been so scared in his life. He wondered if perhaps he could live without flames after all. No! A dragon must breathe fire or he is nothing better than a big, lumpy lizard. Draggle gulped and took off.

Flapping over the volcano, keeping close behind his mother, Draggle didn't dare look down. "Breathe in now!" shouted his mother. Draggle breathed in—and felt as if his whole body was on fire.

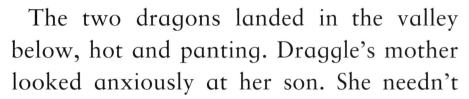

The two dragons landed in the valley below, hot and panting. Draggle's mother looked anxiously at her son. She needn't have worried. The small dragon was himself again. Little flickers of orange fire came out of his nose in a perfectly normal way.

"I hope you've learned your lesson, Draggle," said his mother. "Now, let's go home and have some juniper juice."

"Yes, Mom," replied Draggle. But as they trotted along the valley, one very silly little dragon kept looking at the sparkling water of a little stream rushing along beside them. Luckily, bigger dragons sometimes have very special powers.

"Don't even think about it, Draggle," said his mother.

The Three Little Kittens

The three little kittens,
They lost their mittens,
And they began to cry,
"Oh, Mother dear,
We sadly fear,
Our mittens we have lost!"

"What! Lost your mittens,
You naughty kittens!
Then you shall have no pie.
Meeow, meeow, meeow,
No, you shall have no pie."

The three little kittens,
They found their mittens,
And they began to cry,
"Oh, Mother dear,
See here, see here,
Our mittens we have found!"

"What! Found your mittens,
You darling kittens!
Then you shall have some pie.
Purr, purr, purr,
Then you shall have some pie."

The three little kittens
Put on their mittens,
And soon ate up the pie.
"Oh, Mother dear,
We greatly fear,
Our mittens we have soiled!"

"What! Soiled your mittens,
    You naughty kittens!"
Then they began to sigh,
"Meeow, meeow, meeow,"
    They began to sigh.

The three little kittens,
They washed their mittens,
And hung them out to dry.
    "Oh, Mother dear,
    Look here! Look here!
Our mittens we have washed!"

"What! Washed your mittens?
    You're such good kittens.
But I smell a rat close by.
    Hush, hush, hush,
I smell a rat close by."

Snow White and Rose Red

There was once a poor widow who lived in a cottage. Outside her front door grew two beautiful rosebushes, one with white flowers and one with red. Now, it just happened that the widow had two daughters who were as beautiful as the roses on the bushes. The daughters were called Snow White and Rose Red.

Nobody could have wished for sweeter daughters. They were hard-working, happy, and kind. Everyone loved them. During the day, the two girls helped their mother. In the evenings, they would sit around the fire listening as their mother read aloud to them.

On one such winter's evening, there was a knock on the door.

"Go and open the door, Snow White," said her mother. "It may be someone looking for a place to shelter."

So Snow White opened the door and let out a scream. In front of her stood a huge bear. The bear began to speak: "Don't be frightened. I won't hurt you. I just want to get warm."

"Poor creature," said the girls' mother. "Lie beside the fire. Girls, brush the snow from his coat. He means us no harm."

Before long, the girls lost their fear and played with the bear until it was time for bed. From that night on, the bear came to visit every evening and stayed until morning. The girls and their mother loved him as if he was one of the family.

When spring arrived, the bear said to the girls, "I must go into the forest to guard my treasure from the wicked dwarfs. During the winter the dwarfs stay underground, but now that the weather is warmer they will be out searching for anything they can steal."

Snow White and Rose Red said a tearful goodbye and waved to the bear as he hurried away.

Not long after this, the girls were gathering wood in the forest when they came upon a dwarf. He was jumping around on the ground beside a fallen tree. The tip of his beard was caught in a split in the tree trunk. No matter how hard he tried, he couldn't get away.

"Come and help me, you stupid girls!" screamed the angry dwarf.

"What has happened?" asked Rose Red.

"None of your business, you birdbrained nincompoop," yelled the rude dwarf. "Just get me out of here!"

The girls tried, but they could not pull the dwarf's beard out of the wood. When they could think of nothing else, Snow White took out her scissors and, SNIP, cut off the end of the dwarf's beard.

The moment the dwarf was free, he grabbed a sack of gold and shouted at the girls, "Ugly beasts! Imagine cutting off part of my fine beard." Then, without a word of thanks, he stormed off into the woods.

A few days later, the girls were out fishing when they saw what looked like a huge grasshopper, leaping around beside the river. It was the dwarf once again. He had been sitting beside the river when his beard had dropped into the water and gotten caught in the mouth of a fish. The fish was determined to pull the dwarf into the river. The girls had to do something fast, so once again Snow White drew out her scissors and, SNIP, cut off another bit of the dwarf's beard.

The dwarf was furious. "You nasty spiteful creatures," he cried. "Spoiling a dwarf's good looks!" Then he grabbed a bag of diamonds from among the reeds and disappeared.

59

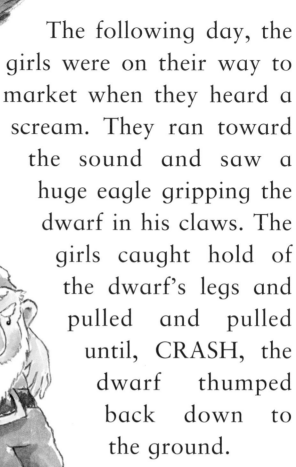

The following day, the girls were on their way to market when they heard a scream. They ran toward the sound and saw a huge eagle gripping the dwarf in his claws. The girls caught hold of the dwarf's legs and pulled and pulled until, CRASH, the dwarf thumped back down to the ground.

Once the dwarf had gotten his breath back, he screeched at the top of his voice, "You clumsy ruffians! How dare you pull me about like that!" Then he grabbed a bag of pearls and disappeared down a hole under a rock.

By now, the girls were used to

60

the dwarf's bad manners and continued on their way to market without giving him another thought. However, on their way back home Snow White and Rose Red ran into him once again. All his treasures were spread out in front of the rock where he had disappeared earlier.

"What are you staring at, you ugly trolls?" screamed the dwarf. He began to put his treasures away. Then, suddenly, with a great ROAR, a huge brown bear appeared in front of the dwarf.

"Forgive me!" cried the dwarf. "Take back all your treasures. Don't eat me, I'm a scrawny little fellow. Eat these plump girls instead."

The bear ignored his words. He picked up the dwarf and threw him down the hole beneath the rock. Then he quickly blocked up the entrance with another rock. The girls were just about to run away when the bear called to them. "Snow White, Rose Red, it's me. Don't be afraid." It was their old friend, the bear.

61

Suddenly, as they turned to greet him, his bear's skin fell away and there stood a handsome prince. "I am Prince Peter," he explained. "That wicked dwarf stole all my treasure and turned me into a bear. Now I have trapped him, and his spell is broken at last."

Soon after this, Snow White married Prince Peter and Rose Red married the prince's brother. They all lived in a grand palace with the girls' mother. The mother even took her two rosebushes with her and planted them in the palace gardens. Every year they grew the most beautiful white and red roses.

The Wind in the Willows

The Mole had been spring cleaning his underground home all morning. His fine coat was splattered with whitewash, and his arms were tired. From outside his underground home, he could hear the spring calling to him. Suddenly, he threw down his brush and cried, "Hang spring cleaning."

He charged out of the house and scrabbled through the tunnel that led to the outside world. At last, POP, the Mole came out into the sunshine.

"This is better than whitewashing," he said to himself, as he ran across a meadow. The Mole ambled along until he came to a river. He'd never seen a river before. He was fascinated by the way the water gurgled and gleamed. Mole sat on the grass and gazed at the bank opposite, until a dark hole caught his eye.

"What a fine home that would make!" he thought. As he continued looking at the hole, something twinkled, then winked at him. It was an eye. An eye that belonged to a little brown face. It was the Water Rat.

"Hello, Mole," called the Water Rat.

"Hello, Rat," called the Mole.

"Would you like to come over?" asked the Rat.

"How?" replied the Mole.

The Rat said nothing, but pulled out a tiny boat and stepped into it.

He was soon at the Mole's side. The Rat held out his paw and helped the excited Mole into the boat.

"I've never been in a boat before," said the Mole.

"What?" cried the Rat. "Well, what have you been doing, then?"

"Is it really that nice?" asked Mole.

"It's the only thing to do," said the Water Rat. "Believe me, my young friend, there is nothing—absolutely nothing—half so much worth doing as simply messing about in boats. I know. Why don't we go down the river together?"

The Mole was overjoyed. "Let's go at once!" he cried.

So the Rat fetched a large picnic basket and they were off.

"What's in the basket?" asked the Mole.

"There's cold chicken," began the Rat "coldham coldbeefcoldpickledgherkinssaladFrenchrolls . . ."

"Stop, stop," laughed the Mole. "It's all too much."

The Rat rowed downstream, while the Mole took in all the new sights and sounds. "What's over there?" he asked, waving a paw at a wood in the distance.

"Oh, that's the Wild Wood. We riverbankers don't go there if we can help it."

"Why not?" asked the Mole nervously.

"Well, some of the rabbits in there aren't bad. And Badger lives right in the heart of it. Dear old Badger. Nobody would mess with him."

"Who would want to mess with him?" asked the Mole.

"You know, the usual—weasels, stoats, and foxes. You can't trust them."

"And what's beyond the Wild Wood?" asked the Mole. "The Wide World," said the Rat. "But I'll never go there, and neither will you if you've got any sense. Ah, here's our picnic spot."

The Rat tied the boat up to the bank and helped the Mole ashore. Soon they were both feasting hungrily on their picnic. Before they had finished, the Mole had met two of the Rat's good friends. First there was the Otter, who declared the Mole a friend of his own before departing. Then there was the Badger, who grunted "Huh, company," before making a hasty retreat.

Toad was also out on the river. He was testing out a brand-new rowboat—and not making a very good job of it. "It's another of his fads," explained the Rat.

"Whatever it is, he soon gets tired of it and starts on something new."

Soon it was time to leave. As the Rat rowed gently home, the Mole grew more and more restless.

"Ratty! Please can I row now?"

"Wait until you've had a few lessons," smiled the Rat.

The Mole was quiet for a minute, then he leaped up and snatched the oars from the Rat.

"You'll turn us over," cried the Rat. And as the Mole swung wildly about with the oars, SPLASH, that's just what happened.

The Mole sank, came spluttering to the surface, then sank once more. Then a strong paw reached out and hauled him onto dry land. It was the Rat. Laughing, he dried the Mole off then plunged back into the water to save the boat and the picnic basket.

When the Mole took his seat in the boat once more, he felt quite ashamed and apologized to his new friend.

"Don't worry about it," said the Rat cheerfully. "You know, I think you should come and stay with me for a while. I'll teach you how to row and swim. You'll soon get used to it. We'll have a wonderful time."

The Mole was so happy that he burst into tears. The Rat pretended not to notice.

When they got home, the Rat lit a cozy fire and told the Mole river stories until suppertime. After a fine supper, a tired and happy Mole went straight to bed.

The following days were similar to Mole's first day on the river. He soon learned to swim and row. Each day, he had fun messing about on the river. Each night, as he drifted off to sleep, he was comforted by the sounds of the river lapping at his windowsill and of the wind whispering in the willows.

The Months of the Year

January brings the snow;
Makes the toes and fingers glow.

February brings the rain,
Thaws the frozen ponds again.

March brings breezes loud and shrill,
Stirs the dancing daffodil.

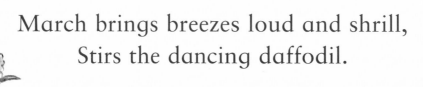

April brings the primrose sweet,
Scatters daisies at our feet.

May brings flocks of pretty lambs,
Skipping by their fleecy dams.

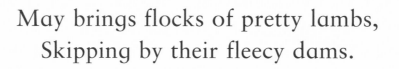

June brings tulips, lilies, roses,
Fills the children's hands with posies.

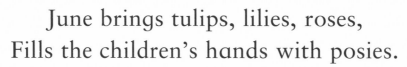

Hot July brings cooling showers,
Strawberries and gillyflowers.

August brings the sheaves of corn,
Then the Harvest home is borne.

Warm September brings the fruit,
Sportsmen then begin to shoot.

Fresh October brings the pheasant;
Then to gather nuts is pleasant.

Dull November brings the blast,
Then the leaves are falling fast.

Chill December brings the sleet,
Blazing fire and Christmas treat.

Sara Coleridge

Thirty Days Hath September

Thirty days hath September, April, June, and November,
All the rest have thirty-one,
Except February alone,
And that twenty-eight days clear
And twenty-nine in each leap year.

The Ghost Who Was Afraid

"I'm not afraid of ghosts!" said Godfrey. "Of course not," said his mother. "Ghosts are not afraid of ghosts. Don't be silly, Godfrey!"

"I'm not afraid at all!" said Godfrey, looking over his shoulder. "But if I weren't a ghost, I might be."

"Well you are a ghost," said his mother. "Now stop walking so slowly or we'll never get home."

"Let's hurry, then," said Godfrey, beginning to run. He pulled his mother along so quickly that she spilled her groceries.

"I'm not afraid of ghosts," said Godfrey, as they passed the haunted mill. "If I was frightened of ghosts, I'd be frightened of myself. Now that would be silly, wouldn't it?"

"Very silly!" said his mother, as they stepped into the deep, dark forest. Here the trees grew so closely together that Godfrey had to glow brightly to see where he was going.

"I'm actually a very, very brave little ghost," said Godfrey.

"Of course you are," said his mother.

Godfrey whistled. He kicked a stone along the path and continued into the forest.

The trees began to hiss and whisper with the wind:

"Whooo is kicking stones at us? Whoooo? Whoooooooooo?"

"Ooooeeeer!" gasped Godfrey as the trees bent over. When their spiky branches snatched at him, Godfrey ran.

"Where are you going?" called his mother. "Wait for me!"

But now Godfrey was no longer pretending to be brave. He knew he was afraid. He was afraid of the trees . . . and the wind . . . and the dark . . . and of ghosts. He was even a little afraid of himself.

Without stopping, Godfrey ran out of the forest and up to Spooky Castle.

"Whooo, whooo, whoooooooooo!"

went the wind, catching up with Godfrey and tossing him into the air.

"Ooooooeeer!" cried Godfrey as he landed on top of Spooky Castle. "Oooooeeer!" said Godfrey again, for here was another ghost. This was not a white, billowy ghost like Godfrey's mother and father. This was a knight in shining armor.

"Stop! Who goes there?" called the knight.

"Me!" gasped Godfrey as the knight clanked toward him.

"Stop! Who goes there?" bellowed the knight again, but he did not see Godfrey. He marched straight through him, into the sky and through the clouds.

"Whooo, whoooooooooo!" went the wind again, and tossed Godfrey into the moat. He landed with a splash and was swept down into the dungeon.

"Oooooeeer!" said Godfrey, for there in the deep, dark dungeon was another ghost. This was not a white, billowy ghost like Godfrey's mother and father. And it was not a knight in shining armor.

This was a little old man. He was dressed in tattered red rags, with chains wrapped around his body.

"Who are you?" he squeaked in a quavery, wavery voice.

"Godfrey," answered the little ghost, "and I'm not afraid, really, even if I am shaking. That is just because I am so cold."

"I have forgotten," moaned the ancient man, "what it's like to be warm. I've been here for hundreds of years. This is my dungeon . . . so go away, I tell you! GO AWAY!"

The old man clanked his chains. Then, suddenly, he grew bigger and bigger, until he filled the dark space.

"Oooooeeer!" cried Godfrey. "Help!"

"Whooo, whoooooooooooo!" went the wind again and sucked Godfrey out through the keyhole. Then the wind rolled Godfrey into a round, white ball and threw him into the haunted bedroom.

"Oooooeeer!" shrieked Godfrey, as he bounced onto the four-poster bed. There, standing in front of him, was another ghost.

This was not a white ghost like Godfrey's mother and father. And it was not a knight in shining armor, nor an old man in chains.

This was a beautiful lady. She was dressed in purple and gold and carried a flickering candle.

"Good evening," said the Purple Lady. She curtsied and took off her head.

"Oooooeeer!" said Godfrey, staring at the head tucked neatly under her arm, smiling at him.

The Purple Lady laughed quietly and whispered, "Don't be

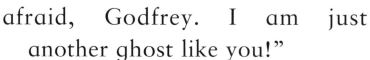

afraid, Godfrey. I am just another ghost like you!"

"I am NOT afraid," snapped Godfrey. "But do you think you could put your head back for a moment? I don't like staring down at you."

"It's very rude to stare, anyway," said the Purple Lady. "A polite ghost like you should know better." But then she sighed and slowly put her head back where it belonged.

"Thank you," said Godfrey.

Just then the wind came down the chimney and swirled Godfrey up in a billow of smoke.

"Whooo, whooooooooooo!" went the wind, blowing Godfrey out of the chimney and into the sky.

"Oooooeeer!" cried Godfrey, as he passed several witches riding on broomsticks. He ducked as the witches cackled and shrieked and pointed at him with their broomsticks.

"Oooooeeer!" cried Godfrey, as a really ugly witch flapped in circles around him. She squealed and swooped until the wind carried Godfrey higher than ever.

"Where are we going?" asked Godfrey.

"To the moon," shrilled the wind.

"No!" cried Godfrey. "I want to go home now, please!"

But still the wind carried him higher and higher.

"Stop it!" cried Godfrey. "Take me home! NOW!"

"All right!" said the wind, sighing. "Spoilsport!"

Then the wind dropped Godfrey. He fell like a stone, down, down, down. He tumbled past the twinkling stars and down to the hill on the edge of the forest.

He fell right back to where his mother was hurrying up the steep forest path. Godfrey landed smack in the middle of his mother's shopping basket.

"Aaah! There now! You've made me spill everything again!" cried his mother. But she was so glad to see Godfrey that she lifted him up and gave him a big hug. And then they went home.

Now Godfrey is glad that things are back to normal again. He has met so many different ghosts that he is no longer afraid of them. In fact, he takes a stroll to the Spooky Castle every evening to play hide-and-seek with his new friends—the knight in shining armor, the old man in the dungeon, and the Purple Lady.

Godfrey has gotten used to his new friends' little habits, such as shouting and marching through walls, rattling chains, and taking off their heads. And he only goes "Oooooeeer!" every now and then, if someone shouts "BOO!" especially loudly.

"I'm not frightened of ghosts anymore," laughs Godfrey the ghost, "only of witches!"

My Shadow

I have a little shadow that goes
in and out with me,
And what can be the use of him
is more than I can see.
He is very, very like me from the
heels up to the head;
And I see him jump before me,
WHEN I JUMP INTO MY BED.

The funniest thing about him is
the way he likes to grow—
Not at all like proper children,
which is always very slow;
For he sometimes shoots up taller
like an India-rubber ball,
And he sometimes gets so little that
THERE'S NONE OF HIM AT ALL.

He hasn't got a notion of how
children ought to play,
And can only make a fool of me
in every sort of way.
He stays so close beside me,
he's a coward you can see;
I'd think shame to stick to nursie
AS THAT SHADOW STICKS TO ME!

One morning, very early,
before the sun was up,
I rose and found the shining
dew on every buttercup;
But my lazy little shadow,
like an arrant sleepyhead,
Had stayed at home behind me and was
FAST ASLEEP IN BED.

Mabel Monster

Mabel wanted to be a singer. But there was one fairly big problem. It wasn't the fact that she was a monster with four arms and three horns. After all, there were other monsters all around her, and some of them looked even stranger than Mabel. No, the real problem was that Mabel could not sing. And when I say could not, I mean she really could not sing in tune at all . . . not a single note.

"It will get better," said Mabel's mother, when her singing baby broke every window in the house.

"She'll grow out of it," said Mabel's father, when his singing toddler made the Christmas tree droop.

"I'd like to order 200 boxes of earplugs, please," said Mabel's grandma on the telephone, when Mabel was still trying to sing at the age of twelve.

Mabel read in a magazine that anyone can become a successful singer if you try, try, and try again.

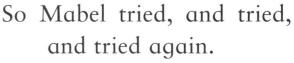

So Mabel tried, and tried, and tried again.

Holding their hands over their ears, all her friends begged her to stop. Her family begged her to take up rollerblading instead. But Mabel was determined.

When Mr. Big, who was famous for making singing stars, came to town, Mabel was filled with excitement.

"I'm going to practice night and day," she cried. "This is my big chance."

"Oh no!" cried her friends, looking sick. But since lots of monsters are green already, it can be hard to notice when they are sick. A sure sign is when purple spots appear on the tongue.

"Oh no!" cried Mabel's family. Her mother booked a last-minute vacation in a faraway place… and strangely forgot to buy a ticket for Mabel.

"Oh no!" cried the other monsters who lived on Mabel's street. They all rushed to go away on vacation, too.

Mabel didn't notice any of this. She could think of only one thing. Wherever she went, she opened her mouth and sang. Whole rooms full of monsters emptied out in seconds.

Mabel knew that her voice was unusual—but surely that was a good thing! Mr. Big was looking for a new star. Mabel practiced her most exciting songs. She was determined to make a big impression on Mr. Big.

If Mr. Big had been a nice monster, someone might

have warned him about Mabel. But Mr. Big, the starmaker, was the most horrible person you are ever likely to meet. He was mean, bigheaded, and very rude. And he had a very peculiar smell, because he liked eating fish heads and chocolate fudge at the same time.

Mabel's big day came at last. Because she was very nervous, her arms began to wiggle and her nose began to run. But Mabel felt as ready as she ever would. She made her way to a theater at the edge of town. When it was Mabel's turn to sing, she clambered onto the stage and peered out at the rows of seats in front of her. Mr. Big was sitting in the front row with some of his helpers.

"Get started" he called.

And so Mabel did. An extraordinary noise came out of her mouth. Can you imagine the noise made by a crowd of squealing piglets? Mabel's noise was something like that.

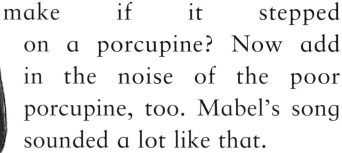

Mr. Big was angry. "Stop!" he yelled.

But Mabel was just hitting her stride. She started another song right away. Can you think of the noise that an elephant might

make if it stepped on a porcupine? Now add in the noise of the poor porcupine, too. Mabel's song sounded a lot like that.

Mr. Big turned red and began to shake. "Shut up!" he howled.

88

Mabel didn't even notice. She had already started her third song.

The theater was filled with the noise of a ballet-dancing hippopotamus crashing through a china shop. With a yell that Mabel would have been proud of, Mr. Big ran out of the theater. He left a nasty trail of green slime behind him.

But out among the seats, someone was clapping. A small green-and-yellow monster rushed up to the stage and shook each of Mabel's four hands in turn.

"Fantastic!" he cried. "Wonderful! Remarkable!" Well, he wasn't really a starmaker. The yellow-and-green monster made cartoons for television.

And he was looking for someone to make the weird and wacky noises that make cartoons so funny.

"Can you do these noises?" he asked Mabel as he handed her a list.

Mabel looked down at the list and read:

"a spaceship landing in a bowl of jello"

"a warthog eating spaghetti"

"a rhinoceros sneezing"

"a giant slug chasing a chicken."

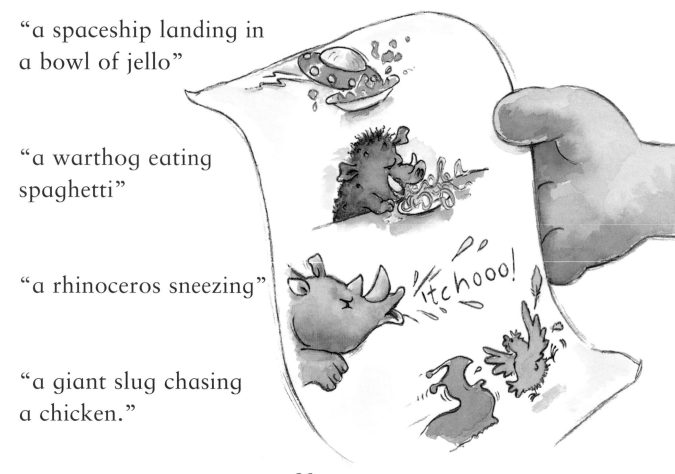

"What could be easier?" she exclaimed.

So the next time you watch a cartoon, shut your eyes and listen to the sounds. You are almost certainly hearing some of Mabel's finest work. But don't try doing it yourself, okay?

How Many Miles to Babylon?

How many miles to Babylon?
Three score miles and ten.
Can I get there by candlelight?
Yes, and back again.
If your heels are nimble and light,
You may get there by candlelight.

Go to Bed, Tom

Go to bed, Tom,
Go to bed, Tom,
Tired or not, Tom,
Go to bed, Tom.

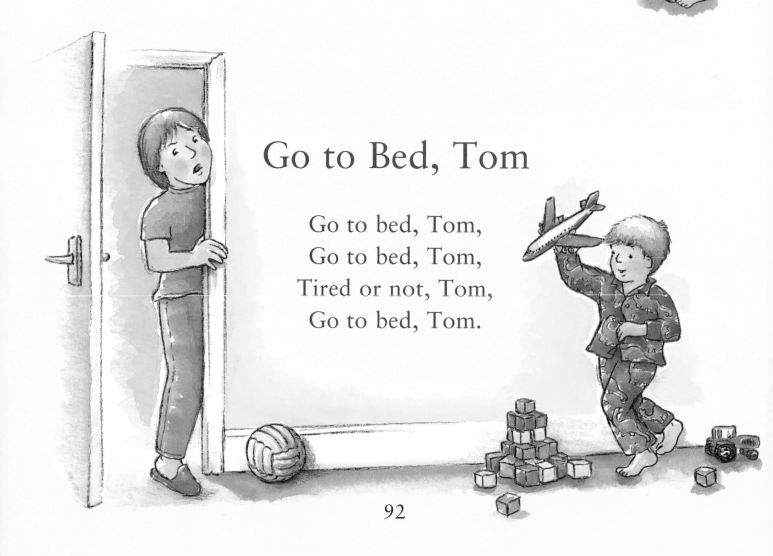

The Moon

The moon has a face like the clock in the hall;
She shines on thieves on the garden wall,
On streets and fields and harbor quays,
And birdies asleep in the forks of the trees.

The squalling cat and the squeaking mouse,
The howling dog by the door of the house,
The bat that lies in bed at noon,
All love to be out by the light of the moon.

But all of the things that belong to the day
Cuddle to sleep to be out of her way;
And flowers and children close their eyes
Till up in the morning the sun shall arise.

Robert Louis Stevenson

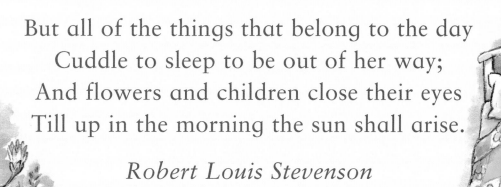